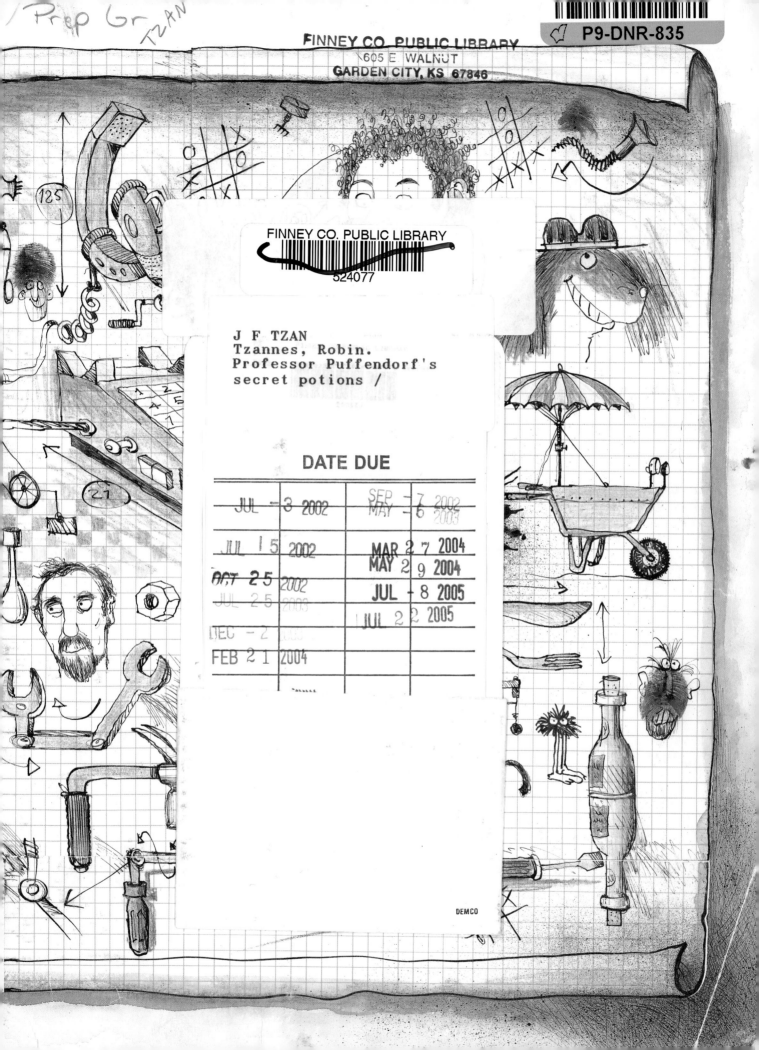

For Sonna—RT

For Jesse Peter Mina, son and heir
to a long line of mustaches—KP

Originally published in England
by Oxford University Press.
Illustrations © Korky Paul 1992
Text © Robin Tzannes 1992

Published in the United States of
America by Checkerboard Press, Inc.,
30 Vesey Street, New York, New York 10007.
ISBN: 1-56288-267-8
Library of Congress Catalog Card Number: 92-71148
Printed in Hong Kong
0 9 8 7 6 5 4 3 2 1

Professor Puffendorf's
SECRET POTIONS

Robin Tzannes and Korky Paul

Checkerboard Press
New York

Professor Puffendorf was the world's greatest scientist.

You probably have some of her inventions in your own home: maybe Unburnable Toast, or a Bananamatic, or perhaps a Smell-o-Telephone.

Professor Puffendorf's laboratory was a wonderful place, full of odd-shaped bottles and tubes and strange-looking machines that hissed and steamed and spluttered and squeaked.

On a cluttered counter in this
laboratory was a cozy cage,
and in this cage lived a guinea
pig named Chip.

He was a friendly little creature, bright and clever.

Professor Puffendorf loved Chip,
and Chip loved her.

Professor Puffendorf's assistant
was a man named Slag, a lazy,
grumbling fellow.

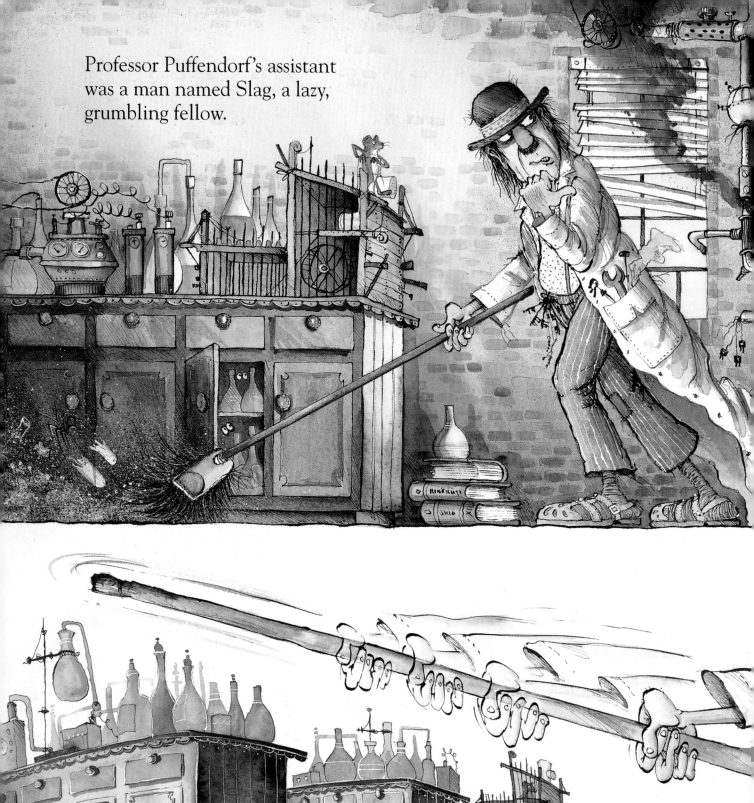

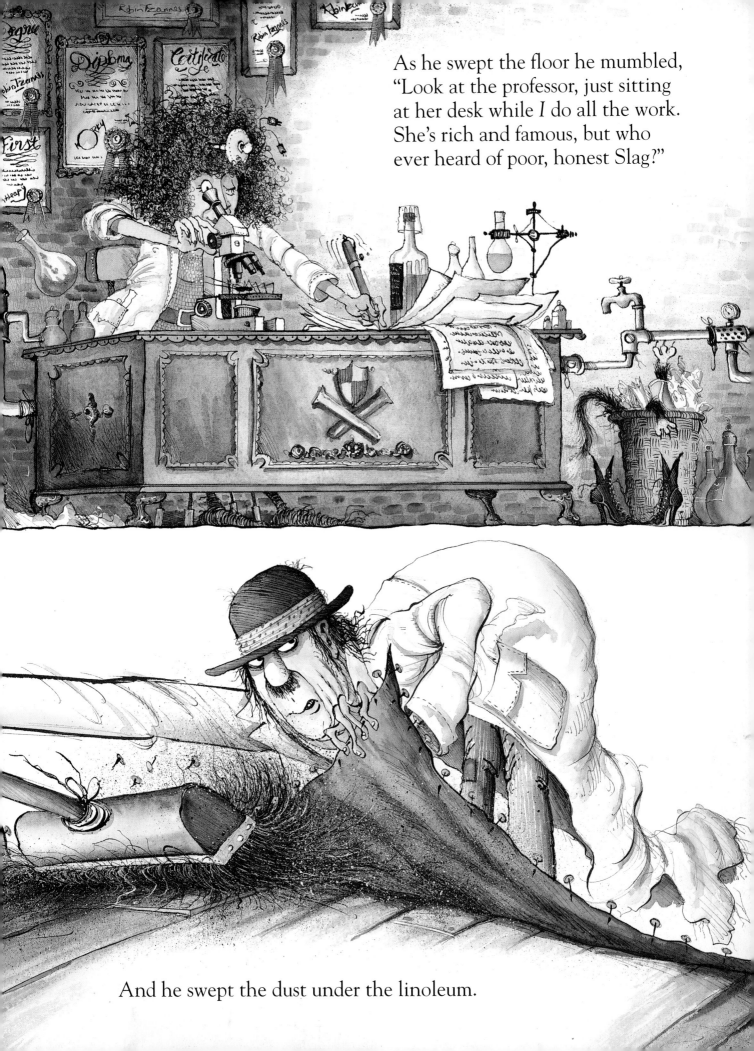

As he swept the floor he mumbled, "Look at the professor, just sitting at her desk while *I* do all the work. She's rich and famous, but who ever heard of poor, honest Slag?"

And he swept the dust under the linoleum.

One day when Professor Puffendorf was going to a conference, she said to Slag, "Please wash all the thistle tubes and dust the Magdeburg hemispheres. And this time, try to remember to turn off the titanium blender when you leave."

Then she put on her hat and went out.

As soon as the professor had gone, Slag jumped into her chair and put his feet up on the desk.

"Ah, yes, *this* is where I belong!" he said, and helped himself to the professor's dish of peppermints.

Suddenly his eye fell on a cabinet
marked TOP SECRET!
   This cabinet was locked with two
padlocks and three combination
locks, and Slag had been told never,
never to open it.

But he forgot that now and
rummaged through the professor's
desk until he found the keys and
combinations.

Soon the top-secret cabinet stood wide open, revealing a colorful row of bottles filled with mysterious potions.

Slag picked one up.
It said: HAIR TODAY. FOR THICK
RED CURLY HAIR INSTANTLY, TAKE
TEN DROPS AND COUNT TO FIVE.

Slag was about to put the bottle to his lips…but he hesitated.
He knew that many of the professor's top-secret formulas had not been tested.

They might not work. They might even be poisonous.

Then Slag had a wicked idea…

...try it on the guinea pig first!

He measured ten drops into
Chip's water bottle.
 "Oh, Chippy," he called.
"Teatime!"

And as Chip drank the potion Slag counted anxiously.

1, 2, 3, 4...5!

It worked!
 Chip's furry little head was suddenly covered with thick red curly hair.

Slag began to prance around the laboratory, clapping his hands and singing, "I'll be rich! I'll be rich! At last I'll be rich!"

He knew that many people would pay a great deal of money for Hair Today.

So Slag decided to steal the formula from Professor Puffendorf.

Slag went back to the top-secret
cabinet to see what else he could
steal.

The next bottle said: SWEET SONG.
FOR A BEAUTIFUL VOICE, SIX DROPS
AND COUNT TO FIVE.

Slag brought the bottle
to Chip's cage and gave
him six drops.

Then he counted.

1, 2, 3, 4, 5...

It worked!

Chip began to sing with a voice so rich and melodious that tears came into Slag's eyes.

Slag could hardly believe his luck.

Why, that cabinet must be *filled* with rare and wonderful inventions—secret potions that would make him rich for the rest of his life.

Now, thought Slag, I'll finally get what I deserve!

He went to try a third bottle.

This one said: BEST WISH. ONE DROP AND COUNT TO FIVE. YOUR HEART'S FONDEST WISH WILL COME TRUE.

Slag's greedy eyes nearly popped out of his head.

"Best Wish! Why, this is all I need. I'll just wish to be rich and famous and…I know! I'll wish to be the boss! No, the mayor! No, no, no! I'll wish to be the *king*!"

But just as he was about to swallow the potion, he remembered…it might not have been tested.

Better give some to Chip first.

Slag looked at Chip with
an evil glint in his eye.
    With trembling fingers
he measured out one
drop, saying, "Make a
wish, boy. Whatever your
little rodent heart desires.
A ton of alfalfa?
A new treadmill?
You name it, Chippy,
and it's yours."

Chip swallowed the potion obediently as Slag counted.

1, 2, 3, 4, 5!

IT WORKED!

When Professor Puffendorf came back that evening, she knew at once what had happened.

The top-secret cabinet was open.

Chip was whistling a magnificent tune as he swept the floor.

And Slag was running on the treadmill.

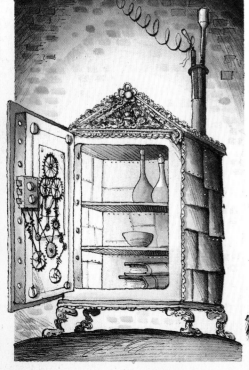

"You're a very silly man," sighed the professor, shaking her head at Slag. "And you got just what you deserved."

She passed a sunflower seed through the bars of his cage.

"But don't worry, my dear. I'm sure I can get you out of this mess."

"But first," she continued, turning to Chip, "I'm famished. Would you care to join me for tea and Unburnable Toast? And then perhaps a game of checkers?"

"Yes, thank you," said Chip. "That would be lovely."

Then he put away his broom, hung up his coat,
and followed the professor out of the laboratory…
remembering to shut off the titanium blender as he left.